Published by Ad Hoc Fiction.
www.AdHocFiction.com

Purchasing Information:
Paperback available from www.AdHocFiction.com

E-book available from all usual outlets.
Printed in the United Kingdom.
First Printing 2022.

ISBN paperback 978-1-915247-14-8
ISBN e-Book 978-1-915247-15-5

Now You See Him

by

Tim Craig

AdHoc Fiction

Für Susi

Contents

Cat Barbecue

In years to come, this is how Dayna and Greg will refer to it and when they do, their friends will give them strange looks and say things like 'you barbecued a cat?' and 'the hell did it taste like?' which will make the two of them roll their eyes. But right now, they are still young and they are here, drinking beer, and their host's cat is weaving in and out of their legs in that seductive, electric way cats do. The hot fat from the grill has yet to drip off the grill onto the cat's back, causing it to dart in terror through the fence out into the road where the laundry truck – driven by a guy called Ricky who is on his phone, but who probably wouldn't have been able to stop in time anyway – has yet to appear. Greg has his strong arm around Dayna, his right thumb teasing the underneath of her breast through the material, the breast that, years from now, will be the source of the trouble not even his strong arm will be able to fix, and he'll wonder if he shouldn't have felt something all those years earlier – maybe even at the Cat Barbecue – because these things, he has read somewhere online, start long before you know. But Dayna will get irritated and say if *I* didn't know back then, how the fuck were *you* supposed to know? Though that's all for the future, and right now it is just a barbecue, not yet even the Cat Barbecue, and the cat is weaving in and out of their legs in that seductive, electric way, and the moon is high and everyone is young.

Parts of my Mother

1.
Once, in a department store, I pulled on my mother's arm and it came off, like she was one of the mannequins. This was an early introduction to the idea that parts of my mother were destined to come off without warning.

2.
I was only a little older when both her legs came off at a summer garden party where she had been drinking wine for some hours. "Your mother has had a bit too much sun," my father explained to us, as he carried her inside like a rag doll, with shiny buttons for eyes.

3.
The next thing to go was her heart. She lost it to Mike, the husband of her colleague at the school where she taught. There was a lot of shouting in our house that week and, soon after, she left for Canada with Mike.

4.
Over the years, postcards would arrive with pictures of grizzly bears and Mounties, telling us things we

didn't want to know, like Mike found a job, and Mike built a treehouse for their new kids and Mike saw a grizzly bear in the garden.

5.
One day a postcard arrived telling us the doctors had found something and they were going to remove some more parts from her, and then the postcards stopped.

6.
A couple of months back I googled her number and called it. It was her voice that answered, but it wasn't her and she didn't know who I was. An older male voice came on.

'You'll have to leave it there, Sport,' it said. 'Too much gone.'

7.
The next postcard was in unfamiliar writing and said she had died. It gave the date of the funeral, which had already passed. On the front was a picture of a grizzly bear rearing up on two legs, and for a moment I wondered if it was the one Mike saw.

Suerte o Muerte

The matador is superstitious. He will not wear yellow on the day of the bullfight; he will not drink lemon tea, nor pass a field of sunflowers without crossing himself. He will not accept the good wishes of his neighbours and, if a small child is heard singing before noon, he will spit on the ground and ask forgiveness of his ancestors. He will not kiss his wife before leaving the house, he will never eat chicken on the day of the fight, and he will not whistle without good reason. He must enter the arena left foot first and greet the bull with the first lines of a poem, preferably by Lorca (although never '*Lament for Ignacio Sánchez Mejias*'). If, after the kill, he throws his *montera* hat over his shoulder and it lands upside down in the sand, legend says it may soon be filled with his own blood. If, driving home from the arena, he sees his wife sitting outside a bar, holding hands with a rival matador, it is thought very unlucky. If he stops the car, gets out and runs them both through with his *estoque*, he will be sent to prison for possibly twenty years. If, while in prison, he hangs himself in his cell, his children will become orphans. If, however, at his funeral, his lover wears purple and throws a single rose onto his coffin while wiping a tear from her left eye with a white *pañuelo*, this is considered a sign of impending good fortune.

Going Down

The elevator is between the twenty-first and the twenty-second floor when the cable snaps, so the passengers have some time to share their life stories before they hit the ground.

'I married too young,' says the woman with the red hair and the butter-soft gaze and the lapel badge which reads 'Baby on Board'.

'I am likeable, and I am loveable,' the middle-aged man in the cream shirt and brown tie says over and over, like a mantra. The red-haired woman notices he has missed a bit of his chin with the razor.

'If I had stayed in Inverkeithing,' says the skinny guy with the safety pin through his eyebrow, 'perhaps people would have bought my photographs.'

'When I was a child of about eight,' says the elderly woman in the blue coat, 'there was a violent lightning storm one night while I slept. My mother woke me up to take out all the metal curlers from my hair.'

'I *am* eight,' says a little girl holding a grubby pink wallaby, 'but I'm going to be nine in December.'

There are two other passengers in the elevator, but they do not have enough time to tell their stories; inevitably in such situations, someone always ends up disappointed.

My Friend, the Fat Somali Man

He is here again, slumped and shirtless, by the all-night Chicky-Chick fried chicken shop, in the alley where the drunks sway and urinate. I think of him as my friend, although we have never spoken. He sits here most days, in his stained pants, eating leftover fried chicken from the cardboard boxes the customers drop, chain-smoking found cigarette butts and drinking from a brown paper bag. He is like a fat chicken on a nest of chicken bones, cigarette butts and empty bottles. It is impossible not to admire my friend the fat Somali man's resolve to die, and yet, in the four years I have watched him sitting there – defiantly alive, in spite of himself – several of my other friends, who did not spend their days slumped against the all-night Chicky-Chick fried chicken shop wall, chain-smoking and drinking from a brown paper bag, have died. I do not know if these other friends were simply unlucky; I do not know if my friend the fat Somali man has inadvertently, improbably, stumbled on the secret of a long and happy life. I do not know if, one marrow-freezing night in the coming winter, he will suffer a fatal cardiac arrest, or be set on fire in his filthy sleeping bag, or be kicked to death by a group of laughing youths. And if so, I do not know who, apart from me, will notice he is gone. I do not how my friend the fat Somali man ended up here in the first place; in this country, in this city, in the piss-soaked alleyway by the side of the all-night Chicky-Chick shop. I do not know his name. I do not know how old he is. I do not know if he is Somali.

The Falling Silent

My mother gave me the small pots and pans, while she took the large ones, and together we went outside to kill the birds.

When we got down to the street, most of our neighbours were already there, gathered under the trees and the lampposts. I saw Mei Zhen – the girl from down the hall – carrying a colander and a ladle. I waved to her, but she turned away.

At the given signal from the loudspeakers, everyone began banging their pans together. Across the city, the sky filled with the noise.

My arms began to tire, but each time I slowed, my mother nudged me to redouble my efforts. I looked up at her and saw the determined expression on her face and the patches of damp on her blue headscarf.

Soon the exhausted starlings began to fall from the sky. Some were dead before they reached the ground, some died at our feet, in the gutters, in the grass in front of the apartment block.

Finally, when I thought my arms could take no more, the loudspeakers gave the signal for the noisemaking to stop.

It came like a great sigh, or the tide sucking back across the pebbles. The silence that followed was even greater than the simple absence of sound, for all the music had been removed from it.

We all went back inside to fetch brooms, with which we set about sweeping the birds into piles by the roadway. The municipal hygiene teams would collect them later in their familiar yellow trucks.

Afterwards, I asked my mother if I could go and play with Mei Zhen, but she told me I needed to help her prepare the dinner. Life isn't all about having fun, she said, banging the pots down on the stove.

Northern Lights

After an hour or so, I decided to ask him about the tooth.

It was dangling from the sun visor on a piece of cotton, and it had a gold filling that occasionally glinted as we passed under the lights.

He reached up and flicked it with his fingernail, setting it dancing back and forth.

'It was my father's,' he said.

Then he grinned.

'The only gold I ever got from him'

Pavel turned to look at the road ahead, his expression serious once more. All three lanes were busy with traffic heading north for the weekend.

He was quiet for a moment or two. Then he shrugged.

'He hit my mother, I hit him. He left. I never saw him again.'

He shifted slightly in the seat.

'I was seventeen.'

He flashed the headlights to allow a Sainsbury's lorry to pull back into the inside lane. The lorry moved across, then toggled its indicators in thanks.

'I found the tooth two days later. It had landed in a flowerpot and I thought I'd better take it with me in case another evil old bastard grew out of it.'

He smiled, and I noticed a flash of gold in his own mouth.

Neither of us said much more after that, and he dropped me off at the next services.

After he'd gone, I stood for a while on the motorway bridge, watching the trail of diamonds and rubies on the wet tarmac.

Full Circle

The young couple are at the very top when the Ferris wheel shudders to a halt. They giggle like the teenagers they are, and joke about staying up there all night and what they might get up to in the dark, under the stars. But when the coloured bulbs go out all around them and the generator noise stops, it's clear they have been forgotten. The next morning, they look down and shout, but nobody comes: the fairground is deserted. After a few weeks, some workmen arrive to erect a high metal fence around the perimeter. The couple watch them leave. As the years pass, they see the rust eating away the dodgem cars below and the weeds growing between the painted horses on the carousel. By the time they reach middle age, the whole site is a derelict wasteland. They ran out of conversation many years earlier so she doesn't bother to tell him she feels a deep sickness in her body, and when she dies it takes him a while to notice. He no longer knows what sad is, so he doesn't know if that's what he is. Soon he, too, dies and this is how the construction crew building the new shopping mall find them, when they switch on the Ferris wheel and give it a spin for old times' sake. One of the workers makes a crude remark, but he is young and has not been with the company long, so the others let it pass.

Splinters

J.
And because it is now the third time she has asked, you come out with it straight: 'she's dead'.

B.
The nurse is big and friendly, exactly the kind you want in the children's department. Her name badge says 'Loretta'.

D.
'Three', your daughter replies, sitting in your lap.

G.
And where's Mummy today? she asks, as if neither of you heard her the first time.

A.
The area around the splinter is angry and red, so you decide to whizz her down to A&E.

E.
And where's Mummy today? She asks. Neither of you answer.

C.
That's a pretty name! And how old are you? She asks.

F.
You look around the room, at the brightly coloured posters and the toys in the play corner. Everything designed to keep your mind off what's wrong.

K.
The look on her face is one of complete and utter devastation. You feel bad for her. But, also, you think she deserves it.

H.
Loretta works quickly and soon the splinter is out. She wipes the tiny finger with antiseptic and stretches a plaster over it.

I.
And where's Mummy today? she says, brightly.

Now You See Him

My father could slip through keyholes, and similar small openings.

Sure, other kids' Dads could do some impressive things, like fix car engines, build sheds or start campfires with a piece of broken glass.

But none of them could disappear without trace from a room where an argument was brewing, like my Dad could.

It was a superpower which served him well through the long years he spent in our too-small house, with his two quarrelling kids and too-angry wife.

Awkward conversations were no match for this legendary escapologist; at the first sign of trouble, he would slide unnoticed between the pages of his hardback.

And as for difficult questions:

"Why does no-one speak to your brother anymore?"
(this was a favourite)
"What does 'gay' mean?"
(this was 1976)

"What would you say if Tina brought home a black boyfriend?"
(this was England in 1976)

"A *gay* black boyfriend?"
(this actually happened)

... he would suddenly remember something that needed to be done in the garage and teleport himself through the wall.

But even Houdini's luck ran out one day.

As my father lay in the metal hospital bed, strapped down like Gulliver, we closed the windows and sealed the exits; for three weeks we bombarded him with small talk, just to keep him from slipping away.

Until the moment we told him we loved him when – in a single bound – he vanished up the coiled, sucking hose of the ventilator, leaving us waiting for the reply, still.

Riddle Me This

(Stop me if you've heard it.) You arrive at a fork in a dusty road, where two bearded men are sitting on either side, smoking hookahs, and you know that one of them always lies and one of them always tells the truth but you don't know which is which and you only get to ask one question to work out the way to Baghdad. But of course, unlike in the riddle, *no-one* always lies and *no-one* always tells the truth. Don't we – most of us – flit between the two, like bees pollinating the lies with truth or the truth with lies? Don't we do it – mostly – to be kind, or at least not to be *un*kind? Adding a dash of lie to an unpalatable truth or a splash of truth to an unpalatable lie? And you park in the car park and light a cigarette to steady your nerves and smoke it under the little glass shelter before crunching the butt into the damp gravel and you walk through the revolving doors and follow the signs to the second floor and the receptionist says please take a seat and you read the two-year-old magazines with yachts or horses or some shit but none of it goes in, and when your name is called you walk into the small, stuffy office and there are two bearded men there, one perched on the cupboard on the left and one sitting in a swivel chair on the right, and they smile and say hello, and you know that one of them always lies and one of them always tells the truth but you don't know which is which and you only get to ask one question to work out the way to Baghdad.

The Poor Widder

She kilt her first husband with an axe from the shed. She kilt her second with a knife from the drawer. She kilt her third with poisoned stew. She kilt her fourth with a rock from the stream. She kilt her fifth with sarcasm and her sixth with pity. She kilt her seventh with the smell from between her legs, and her eighth with the hope for better. Her ninth, tenth and eleventh died of suffocation, the coroner said. Her twelfth was the coroner hisself, and she kilt him with curiosity. She pushed her thirteenth in the sea and her fourteenth downstairs. She hanged her fifteenth from the old oak and ate her sixteenth alive. Her seventeenth was the only one she ever loved and after she split his head open with the poker from the fire, she cradled him in her arms the whole night through, and sang him The Curragh of Kildare.

The B of the Bang

There's a scene in 'North by Northwest', just before Eva Marie Saint shoots Cary Grant, where a little kid in the background – an extra – presses his fingers in his ears. Like he knows there's going to be a bang. Because he *does* know there's going to be a bang. Because this is maybe the fourteenth or fifteenth take. And somehow no-one notices – not the editors, or continuity, or Hitchcock himself – so he makes the final cut of the movie. And no-one knows this boy's name, but if he's still alive today at seventy or eighty then I wonder if he still knows just before things go *bang*! Does he brace just before the jar of pickles slips from his wife's hand? Does he know to pull her away from the curb just before the runaway pickup rounds the bend? Does he slump into his chair before the phone even rings and his daughter tells him her diagnosis? Did he ever pull someone clear of falling masonry? Does he answer questions before they're asked? Or did he, instead, keep his small superpower quiet all these years, knowing how the Government or the Military or Big Pharma might exploit it? Such that, now, he only uses it in extreme circumstances, for example to stand up and leave the room just before the hard words start. Like my father sometimes would when my mother got going, his fingers pressed firmly in his ears, ready for the bang.

Incompatible.

'This is not a day of celebration for the Church.'

Thus spake the priest, as the young couple looked up, and St Bernadette looked down.

To underline his point, no sound came from the organ and no hymns were sung; in the tarnished brass vases which lined both sides of the nave like a guard of dishonour, no lilies were permitted to stand.

Afterwards, with no kind words of blessing to send them on their way, the bride and groom stood before the closed doors of the church for a single stolen snap.

No matter that, for the next sixty years of marriage, they would prove as close as a couple could be.

No matter that each would know what the other needed before they knew it themselves.

No matter that they would always hold hands on their walks, even as those walks grew shorter and slower.

That she had been taught Christ was like the bread, while he had been told Christ *was* the bread, proved enough in the eyes of the Church to make them forever incompatible.

Today, as I place daffodils beside the stone which bears both their names, I wonder how they did it, nonetheless. And I picture their hands beneath the soil, seeking out the other's, in quiet defiance still.

The Woodman and the Tree

If a woodman accidentally chops his leg off in the forest and there is no-one there to hear it, does he make a scream?

Does the tree laugh?

Pool

In Malta on holiday Christa challenges Carl to submerge himself in the perfect blue of the swimming pool at the villa they are renting for the week and to see how long he can stay there and never one to duck a challenge Carl lowers himself into the water takes a deep breath and drops to the bottom where he crosses his legs and sits down on the smooth tiles and begins to count to himself and as he does so he looks around and finds the blue of the pool so restful he wishes he could stay here away from the arguments with Christa and the emails from work and the local girl who comes to clean the pool twice a week and who Carl has a thing for which means when she bends over with the net to scoop out the insects he is obliged to roll over on the sun lounger to disguise his arousal and if he looks up he can make out Christa standing at the edge of the pool staring at him from a different world the way she did when the nurse told them there was no heartbeat and he opens his mouth and allows a few bubbles of air to rise to the surface of the pool and burst in the breathless heat of the day.

A Bomb by any Other Name

The bomb does not know it is a bomb.

'Perhaps I am a bird,' it says, trying to flap its shiny wings.

'No, you are not a bird,' say the birds, as the bomb whistles past them through the clear, blue sky.

'Then maybe I am a beautiful butterfly,' says the bomb, proudly, admiring the bright colours painted on its sleek sides.

'No, you are definitely not a butterfly,' says a butterfly, narrowly avoiding the pointed tip of the falling bomb.

The bomb thinks hard for a moment. (Thinking is not the bomb's strong suit.)

'In that case, perhaps I am a child's birthday balloon?' it says. 'That would explain these big numbers printed on my body.'

'I can assure you, you are *not* a balloon,' says a passing hot air balloon, a little sniffily.

The bomb looks down at the bustling city below, twinkling in the sunshine. Now it can make out whole blocks and tall buildings, and soon buses and cars, and even individual people, going about their lives. Everything is getting bigger and bigger very quickly.

'Well,' says the bomb, furrowing its steel eyebrows. 'If I am not a bird, a butterfly, or a balloon, what on earth am I?'

In the street below, a young woman wearing a red baseball cap is buying a hot dog from a street vendor. As she takes the half-empty mustard bottle, she feels a sudden shadow pass over her, as if a cloud has moved across the sun.

She looks up and screams, '*A bomb!*'

'Thank you!' says the bomb, with a huge wave of relief which is felt for hundreds of miles in every direction. After all, self-knowledge is a wonderful thing, however late in life one may acquire it.

The Unwelcome Collection

It began in such a small way she didn't even notice.

One of her friends went on a day trip and brought her back a gift: a tiny, ceramic Tudor cottage.

'Thank you,' said the woman although as far as she was concerned, it was just one more knick-knack she would need to dust.

A second friend popped by and saw the little cottage sitting on the mantelpiece. She made a mental note and, later in the year, returned from holiday with a small package taped up in bubble wrap. It was a tumbledown Norman church.

"I thought it would go well with the cottage," she said.

'Thank you,' said the woman, forcing a smile.

Successive birthdays and Christmases brought more of the cutesy houses, pubs, shops and barns, until there was no room left on the mantelpiece for anything BUT the sprawling array of miniatures.

In time, their number expanded onto the shelves of the bookcase and took over the windowsill. Some of the buildings even made it out into the garden shed, where they competed for space with the cobwebs and broken flowerpots.

'I'm afraid there's not much now we can do to stop the spread,' said the young man, fiddling with his pen. 'Once it's left the original site, all we can really do is try to manage the symptoms.' He smiled. 'I'm very sorry.'

The woman reached out and squeezed his hand.

'Thank you,' she said. And meant it.

BREAKING

He brings her bad news stories, the way the cat brings her dead mice – as a token of love. She listens, tuts in the right places and flips the pancakes. What can she say in response to such unremitting sadness! After breakfast, he follows her around the house, reading from the morning paper while she cleans the bath, scrolling through the newsfeeds while she vacuums the stairs, broadcasting body counts through the toilet door. It is sweet how he does this, she thinks – reminding her that however unhappy she is living here with him, she would be much more unhappy out there, in a world of wars, famine, murders and disease. His way of saying, please don't leave me. And she won't – not yet. Not so long as he keeps bringing her the bad news, offered like fine chocolates, tied up in a bow.

A Manchester Lament

For John Foden. 1852-1865

Although we yearn for the details, we know that if we hurry Mary now, the shuttle of words may fly from the frame, and the story untangle; yet we cannot help interrupting her.

'And was that the worst? The boy's cry, which they say was heard even above the clattering of the loom?' asks Helen, lowering her voice, though there are none but us here in the kitchen.

'No, not that,' says Mary.

'Then was it the sight of his head, crushed between roller beam and carriage?' says Anna, forcing her palms together to simulate the pressure.

'Not that either,' says Mary, inspecting an oily fingernail.

'The limbs, wrenched from his body and thrown to the floor?' says Ethel, casting her arms wide and almost dropping the sleeping baby in her lap.

'No.'

‘The screams of the mother, summoned from the carding room,’ says Peg, clutching her throat to feel them for herself.

‘Not these,’ says Mary, ‘though I shall never be free of hearing them.’

She reaches for the glass of porter with her good arm and raises it to wet her lips, the better to thread the story.

But Emma, the youngest of us here – with only the tip of one slender finger gone – cannot contain herself any longer.

‘If it was not the lad’s cry, or his head, or the limbs, or his mammy, then what was it?’ she half-shouts.

The older woman fixes her with a look.

‘The worst,’ she says, ‘is that the loom was only stopped long enough to pull his body clear. And afterwards, we carried on as before.’

There is a silence, then Ethel’s baby starts to cry.

‘Wisht, little man!’ says Mary. ‘Your shift will begin soon enough.’

Swingers

The two lovers are sitting on a bench in front of the Monkey House. They have been sitting here for half an hour without speaking, although this is perhaps not surprising, as neither is the lover of the other. Lover A – let's call him – is waiting for Lover C, while Lover B, sitting beside him, is waiting for Lover D. A fact unknown to Lover A is that Lover C was killed by a stray bullet an hour ago, during a botched bank robbery, and for many years after today Lover A will feel guilty about the angry texts he sent Lover C demanding to know why she is so late, and without explanation. Meanwhile, Lover D is supposed to be meeting Lover B but has spent the morning having sex with Lover E in her expensive apartment overlooking the river and has lost track of time. Lover A will eventually turn and say something to Lover B, probably just to break the boredom, probably something to do with the monkeys: 'they're so human, aren't they?' Lover B will just smile and nod politely; the last thing she wants is to get drawn into a conversation with some weirdo sitting on a bench outside the Monkey House, even if he seems friendly enough and not the kind of guy to screw around with Lover E in her expensive apartment overlooking the river the way she knows Lover D does. Lover A sends another angry text to Lover C, Lover B's phone pings with a message from Lover D, saying there has been a flood at the shop, which is why he is running late. Lover E kisses his naked back and lights a cigarette. Lover B and Lover A watch in silence as a monkey presses its arse to the glass.

Hier

Sur l'autoroute A9
Sept personnes
Ont été tuées

is the poem our French professor gave us to critique, in our first seminar in his austere rooms. And we, young and eager to impress, fought over it like baby birds over a worm, pulling it and stretching it and deconstructing it.

But the joke was on us. This was no poem, the professor told us after some minutes, the hint of a serpent's smile playing at the edge of his mouth. He had copied it from *Le Monde* the previous day, and merely set it out like a poem. And we – feeling embarrassed now, and stupid – had fallen for it.

Except we hadn't, he said, his grin widening. Because who is to say it wasn't a poem, after all? Perhaps what made it one was what we brought to it? In interpreting it thus, had we not *made* a poem from that which was not? So now we felt stupid and brilliant at the same time.

But that still left the seven people killed on the A9 motorway. I wanted to know who they were, their names and their ages. Most of all, I wanted to let them know that – because I now, at eighteen, finally understood exactly what a poem was – their tragic deaths had not been in vain.

Day of the Knife

After the teenager is stabbed to death, the police search the park for the murder weapon. But the knife is too clever for them; it crawls under a bush and waits until the coast is clear. After everyone has gone, it slides out and slips under the fence. A fox, rummaging in a heap of takeaway boxes, spots it and gives chase. The knife, though, is too quick for it; it jumps into the canal and washes itself clean. It swims downstream for a short distance before climbing out and drying itself on a patch of grass. Tired from all the excitement of the day, it lies down in a dark alleyway to rest amongst a pile of binbags. But the glint of the moonlight on the knife's blade catches the attention of a vagrant who thinks maybe he can sell the knife for enough money to buy a bottle of vodka. As he bends down unsteadily to pick it up, the knife wakes up and darts between his feet. It skitters back out of the alleyway and, keeping to the doorways and shadows, makes its way along the High Street to the bus depot, where it squeezes through a cracked window. Once inside the unlit building, it prises open the door of one of the empty buses and, with its sharp point, pulls itself upstairs. It falls into a deep sleep on the back seat and dreams the kind of dream only a knife can.

The motion of the bus wakes the knife up. It looks out through the window, at the tops of the neat, suburban trees passing by in the morning sunshine. After a while the bus stops, and the knife hears a group of schoolboys clattering noisily up the stairs, laughing and shouting and arguing. The knife lies motionless on the seat. And waits.

The Wrong Boyfriend

My aunt asked my father to pick up her new boyfriend from the station and bring him home to meet their parents. My father had other plans but he was too polite to say. He had never met the boyfriend so when he arrived at the station, he approached the young man standing underneath the clock and asked him if he was my aunt's boyfriend. He wasn't, but he was too polite to say. So my father drove him back to the house where my aunt and grandparents were waiting. As soon as they walked in, my aunt saw that the man wasn't her boyfriend, but she was too polite to say. They sat down to dinner and told stories and, all in all, had a wonderful evening. My grandparents didn't like the way the new boyfriend chewed with his mouth open, or his German accent, but of course they were too polite to say. In time, my aunt and the new boyfriend were married (the new boyfriend was Jewish, while she was Catholic, but he was too polite to say). My aunt suggested they go and live in Berlin; she'd always wanted to see Berlin and of course her new husband spoke the language so might find work as a translator for the American forces. Berlin was the last place her new husband – my uncle – wanted to go and live but he didn't want to make a fuss, so they moved to Berlin. One day while living there he went to the dentist and although the dentist gave a different name, my uncle recognised him as a former neighbour who had turned his entire family over to the Nazis. He confronted the dentist with this fact, but the old man was too polite to say. So my uncle strangled him with the leather belt of the dentist's drill, and walked out of the surgery, politely raising his hat to the receptionist. The police issued a description of the suspected murderer of the dentist and soon came to arrest my uncle. They sat him down in the interview room and asked him straight out if he'd done it. Years later, I asked him what he told them. But he was too polite to say.

Eggs

When she opens the box there is a feather on one of the eggs and she doesn't like that, not one bit. *Too Much Information*. Not that she's naïve; she is a forty-seven-year-old woman with two kids and she knows where eggs come from, for Christ's sake. She just doesn't want to be reminded, in case it sets off a whole other string of memories – like firecrackers – from the other side of things where she prefers to keep them, and – oh-oh, too late – because now she is back in 1984 or '5 on holiday in – where? Benidorm? – and her father is clambering over her to get into the other seat on the pedalo, which is rocking precariously from side to side in the turquoise water, and as she looks up, one of his testicles slips out of his red and white striped, too-tight swimming trunks and it is dark and hairy, the size of an egg, and of course she knows men have these things, and what they're for – she herself is testament to it. *Testament*! Isn't even the word related to testicles? She has read this somewhere about Greeks or Romans swearing an oath while holding their testicles. Or this a myth? Oh, how she wishes things would know to stay where they belong: on the chicken, in the swimming shorts, in the toga.

'Em, you are so quaint!' Rod said to her last night when she insisted, as usual, on turning out the light before they made love.

She takes two eggs from the box, rolls them in her hand to feel their heft, then smashes them hard on the side of the bowl.

Ungrateful

His mother gave up everything for him
His mother worked her fingers to the bone for him
His mother made sure he had the opportunities she never had
His mother sacrificed her own ambitions for him
His mother made sure there was always food on the table
And clean clothes to wear and a roof over his head
His mother slaved over a hot stove for him
His mother gave him the education denied her
And chose his friends carefully for him,
And later, his girlfriends and wives, too.
For him, his mother would not be like *her* mother.

And in return, he wished only that she might be happy.
And for that, she never forgave him.

Petting Time

The old people enjoy petting the dog the nice young man brings to the Old People's Home on Tuesdays. But soon they tire of it and tell the nice young man that Labradors are fine as far as it goes but life in the Old People's Home is so dull they would prefer him to bring something a little more exciting to Petting Time next week. So the following Tuesday the nice young man brings them a goat, and the old people are very happy, and pet it and feed it stale chocolate biscuits when the young man's back is turned. 'That was very nice,' they say, at the end of the visit, 'but for Petting Time next week please bring a different animal.' So the next week the nice young man brings a spiny anteater but no sooner has he entered the lounge where they sit and doze in their pink armchairs than the old people say 'How are we meant to pet that, you stupid boy? Next week, bring us something better' so the nice young man has a think and the following Tuesday he brings a Highland Cow and leads it around the lounge for the old people to pet, and the old people grudgingly admit that the Highland Cow is indeed a fine animal to pet, with its docile nature and its long shaggy hair, but the smell is frankly, repulsive, and if they open the window all the heat will be let out, and does the nice young man want them all to freeze to death? And the young man sighs and says he doesn't know if he will come any more but the old people bat their eyelashes and pout their lips so sadly the nice young man rolls onto his back and puts his arms and legs into the air and the old people pet him and pet him and pet him.

Apple Green Coat

In the newspaper this week there is a story of the kind which comes around with a certain regularity in the quiet months. An unknown woman has been found dead in her apartment, sitting in an armchair. The report speculates she may have been there, undiscovered, for as long as two years, and goes on to provide the unexpected detail of an apple green coat she was found wearing. As if this could help jog the memories of friends or family who – although having forgotten the woman herself – might yet remember the coat.

The article provokes the hand-wringing reaction such articles invariably do – and are designed to. 'Has our society sunk so low that a woman can die unnoticed amongst us?' the editorial asks? 'Are our cities now so unfriendly that not one of her neighbours thought to check on her welfare in two years?'

But it is still the apple green coat I return to. Had she put it on in order to go out; perhaps to meet a lover? Or had she just come back in, exhausted from the shops or the office, and collapsed into the chair just to 'give herself five minutes' before embarking on the demands of the evening?

And I disagree with the conclusions of the newspaper, and those of the citizen-moralists in the online comments, that the woman's story is necessarily an indictment of the city. Is it not at least possible she came here precisely in order to escape the suffocating scrutiny of a village or small town? And, having at last achieved the anonymity she craved, she buttoned up her apple green coat, sat down in her favourite chair, and whispered, 'Now'.

Peacocks

The place they are renting has gardens where white peacocks roam freely. He wishes she would stop feeding them, and tells her so. She feeds them some more. Soon the birds come to spend afternoons on the porch with them, and evenings in the house while the couple watch TV. At night, they hop up onto the frame of the bed and nest on the sheets. He cannot sleep, watched like this. In the moonlight, in the room, the peacocks stand like question-marks at the end of his own thoughts: Why did we come here? Why must we stay? Why did we marry? By the sixth day he can stand it no more: he tells her he is leaving. He packs his case, jumps in the hire car and speeds away down the dirt track in the direction of the city. Once the dust from the wheels has settled, she pours herself a mint tea, cuts herself a slice of cake, and takes an iron chair out onto the soft lawn. The peacocks gather around her, waiting for the usual crumbs. But she has no further need for them, and tells them so.

Profuse

He knew he had fucked up big time. No lawyer would have taken the case. And all he could think of to try to fix it was the caveman's apology: flowers. But in his rush to order them from the website, his finger must have slipped and added an extra couple of zeros, or five, because the next thing he knew she was calling him asking him why the hell a bouquet the size of Portugal had been delivered to the doorstep? He jumped in a cab and went straight over, and when he got there, he saw roses pressed up to the front window and tulips exploding out of the letterbox and gerberas poking out of the roof like the multi-coloured brush of a chimneysweep. He fought his way through the peonies on the porch and into the hallway, calling her name. The scent was overpowering and at first he was afraid he might faint. He shouted her name again and he heard a rustling sound from a nearby hundredweight of lilies and her face suddenly appeared, striped with dark orange pollen. Before he could say anything she had pulled him into the undergrowth and torn off his trousers. They made earnest and insistent love right there on a bed of carnations and after they had finished, they lay side by side, smoking and staring at the canopy of dahlias overhead. He reached out and lazily teased the petals of a nearby Black-eyed Susan, imagining foolishly he had been forgiven.

The Cake of her Life

And the baby stood on the kitchen chair singing, "Do you know the Muffin Man?" over and over as the woman mixed the ingredients in the bowl.

To the flour and eggs and the baking powder and the margarine, the woman added her car keys and her purse. And the baby laughed and clapped its hands. Next, the woman added her mobile phone and her watch, and a tampon, and her Burt's Bees lip balm. And she gave the baby a handful of coins to drop into the bowl too, and the pair of them took it in turns to push the money deep into the mixture with the wooden spoon.

Then the woman dipped her little finger into the mixture and held the finger out to the baby to suck and asked the baby if the cake needed some more sugar. And the baby laughed so the woman added more sugar, as well as her cigarette lighter and her Visa card and her little pocket diary and a ring and a photograph of the baby when it really was a baby. And when these were all stirred in, she tipped the whole mixture into the cake tin, and smoothed it over with the spoon and popped it in the oven and closed the door.

She picked up the baby and put it in the buggy and fastened the straps and pushed the buggy from the kitchen and down the hall and through the front door and up the path and out of the gate and along the pavement. She leaned over with her upside-down face and told the baby they were going for a walk and that they wouldn't stop until they got to Drury Lane, if at all. If at all.

Post Mortem

Soon afterwards – it seems like only a heartbeat – he is led into a different room with the same blonde pine furniture and hushed blue carpet, where a cadaverous doctor sits behind a blonde pine desk and gestures with a thin white hand to a blonde pine chair. And, having tipped up a noisy envelope of personal effects for his inspection – a wedding ring, a bracelet, small earrings, lipstick – comes straight out with it: 'And who, now,' she says, in a pinched Aberdeen accent, 'will look after the child?'

As if it would not be him! As if he might now wish to deposit his young daughter in some poorhouse, or at a baby hatch, with a cursory note tucked into her swaddling.

He jumps up from the chair and grabs the doctor's hand. 'Come!' he says, dragging her out of the blonde pine office, along the plush corridor and down the marble stairs; he pulls her to his car and drives her back to the house. 'See!' he says. 'We have hot and cold running water and food in the cupboards, and clothes to wear and books to read!'

But the doctor stares at him, incredulous. '*You*?' she says. '*You* will look after the child?' And she laughs so hard the walls shake and the wine glasses shatter and the pictures fall from the wall. And he seizes the doctor and kisses her on her cold white cheek and waltzes her around the room until they are both so dizzy they may fall over, because for all the kindness he has received these past months, no gift was ever as great as this.

SVU 762

was the registration of the scooter they were riding under a Sunday morning blue sky when the baker's van ignored the junction and drove not just at them and into them, but through them and over them. Somehow, she was thrown clear and escaped with just a broken wrist, but he was taken to hospital where the doctors said it was quicker to list the parts of him that weren't fixable rather than the parts that were. And eventually the priest was called to administer last rites, but in spite – or perhaps because – of this, one morning he awoke from the coma and leapt up in the bed, pulling out all the tubes with a pop! pop! pop! and calling his wife's name, convinced she was being held hostage by the Russians, this being at the time of the Bay of Pigs and the two events having fused together in his head as inseparably as the ribs in his chest.

But if you were to run the film backwards, you would see him being carried out of the hospital, placed in the ambulance, and rushed at speed to the junction on Yew Tree Road where they would place him in the unrecognisable, mangled wreckage of a scooter which would immediately reconstitute itself and, just a few weeks later, carry the young couple, in reverse, all the way from Manchester, and over the Alps to Venice and back again without either of them sustaining so much as a scratch.

'If it wasn't for the bad luck, I wouldn't have any luck at all,' he would say in later years, laughing until his ribs got the better of him, when he would hunch full forward in the armchair, as if bracing for impact.

The Grand Finale

Even by his own high standards, The Great Fantoni's world tour had been a triumph. The crowds had turned out in their thousands to welcome him wherever he went and the newspaper reviews had proclaimed the show his best yet.

When the magician finally arrived home, he handed his coat and jacket to his wife and announced that he would be going straight to bed.

Mrs Great Fantoni wished her husband a good night and, although she was tired herself, said that she would unpack his things for him before retiring.

After he had gone up, she dragged his large, monogrammed trunk down the hallway and into the sitting room. There, she undid the gold clasps, lifted the heavy lid, and took out a hinged leather portmanteau.

From this, she removed a vintage suitcase, which she noted still bore the faded destination label from their honeymoon. Inside the suitcase was a hand-tooled crocodile skin valise, which, in turn, held an old canvas rucksack.

Scrunched up in the rucksack was a blue sports holdall, from which she pulled a plastic supermarket bag containing her husband's cheap floral wash bag.

She unzipped the wash bag and took out his orange plastic toothbrush holder. She popped this open to discover an empty foil condom packet from which, with a flourish – and the sound of triumphant applause ringing in her ears – she extracted the children, the house and half the money.

Two Stories About an Affair That Didn't Happen

I heard a story about a woman – let's call her my Mother – who had an affair with a photographer friend with just one lung. Although she denies it. In this story, the woman takes pity on the photographer friend because of his one lung, and this is why she has the affair. (There may be other reasons, but this is the one given.) In time, this woman's husband – let's call him my Father – finds out about the affair and, one night, after a big argument, chases the one-lunged photographer down the street and out of both their lives forever.

But this isn't that story. This is a story *about* that story; about how, one day, years later, a family friend who knew the details told me the story – which I had never heard before – and how, when I asked the woman in the story about it over dinner one night, she looked me straight in the eye and denied it.

So, to be clear, there are two stories, and this is the second one. And in this one, you can see that some names from the first story have been changed to protect the identities of the people involved, even though it is many years after the events in question, and even though the woman in the first story – let's call her my Mother – died some years ago.

Although she denies it.

On the Occasion of a Visit to the Aquarium, and Some Advice Proffered

Shay's wife Kath says the fish in the aquarium are not happy. Shay asks her how she can tell; she says it's obvious.

'Why don't you clean your fucking fish tanks?' Kath says to the woman in the ticket booth on the way out.

'Why don't you clean your fucking mouth?' the woman says.

Shay reflects on the fact that, sometimes, there are advantages to a life spent protected by a thick pane of grimy glass.

Body Copy

When Steeny's wife dies young, he is too upset to compose the inscription for her gravestone, so his mother offers to help. 'You weren't married all that long' she says, 'so maybe we should just have her maiden name' 'OK,' Steeny says. 'And as well as her age, why don't we include her height? She was very short after all, and people might not know that otherwise' 'You're right,' says Steeny, blowing his nose on the handkerchief his mother has given him. 'Do you know what she always reminded me of?' his mother says, brightly. 'A little pink fairy! Perhaps we could get them to make one and put on the top of the stone?' 'Good idea,' says Steeny, staring out of the window towards the rainy park, where he was once mugged by two twelve-year-old girls, although he didn't report it. 'As a final touch,' his mother says, 'we could add some big lights around the outside, like in a Hollywood actor's dressing room. She was such a little star, after all!' Steeny blows his nose again and thanks her for all her help; he doesn't know what he would have done without her, he says – his voice muffled by the handkerchief.

The next year, Steeny's father dies. His mother texts Steeny a photo of the headstone she has had made. On it is carved just his father's name and a date. 'Elegant and classy,' his mother writes in the accompanying message. 'Just like the man himself!'

Planes, Horses and Planes

I

We haven't even taken off yet, and I am already clammy with fear.

Don't say that thing, I tell her.

- What thing?
- The thing you always say. About horses.
- More people are kicked to death by horses every...
- There – you said it, I say.
- Well, it's true.

At the macro level, perhaps. But when you are actually ON a plane, the odds narrow somewhat.

The intercom crackles into life.

- Hi everybody. This is the Captain. Sorry for the slight delay. It's just taking a bit of time to board our last passenger.

I look out of the window. On the tarmac, three burly stable-hands are struggling to drag a roped horse towards the steps of the aircraft. The horse shies and kicks, and a hat belonging to one of the men blows off and skitters away down the runway.

II

We are on horseback, overlooking the canyon. I don't like horses. They scare me. My hands are clammy holding the reins.

- Don't say it, I say.
- Say what?
- Say the thing you always say. About aeroplanes.
- But it's true, she says. More people are killed in aeroplane crashes every year than...
- Are you sure it's not the other way round? I say.

She scrunches up her nose in that way I like.

- Maybe, she says. I'll have to google it.

I look up, shielding my eyes against the low afternoon sun. There are flames, and a cloud of smoke in the sky. In the middle of the cloud is a black shape, getting bigger very quickly.

The horse paws the red sand and whinnies.

Cut Outs

Everyone needs a hobby, especially single men of a certain age, and mine is buying up old photographs from flea markets and garage sales and the like. I have no care nor judgement for the aesthetic merits of the photographs themselves; in fact, I would buy them by weight if they were sold that way. My interest begins and ends with the people pictured. I take them home, carefully cut them out from their backgrounds and then have them perform for me in the cardboard box theatre I have built expressly for the purpose. These productions are entirely improvised and the results can be surprising. Last Sunday, for example, I introduced a homely looking mother of three to a stern-faced military man from the Great War. They began a passionate affair immediately, as if the enforced celibacy of decades spent lying in the bottom of a rusty Highland Shortbread tin had wound them both tight as springs. 'Oh! Oh!' she cried, as he pulled her to his sepia tunic, 'Must you go and fight? Can you not stay here with me, in our two-tone cream-and-brown caravan in 1974 Rhyl?' To which he replied, with a twirl of his waxed moustache, 'God,

King and Country are summoning me, my Darling, and only the coward can refuse the call.' It was a heart-breaking scene which genuinely moved me, but I should be clear: few performances will be this successful. More often than not, the characters will simply stand there in their wedding dresses, scuba gear or gardening outfits, refusing all entreaties to interact with each other: smiling, wooden, mute.

That's All There Is, There Ain't No More

Cribbage is a traditional card game for two players, for example a father and his son who haven't spoken for six years, in which the object is to score 121 points while avoiding eye contact. Cribbage is a game sometimes played by a father and his adult son, where the wooden scoring board serves as a proxy for difficult conversation. Cribbage was invented by the seventeenth century poet Sir John Suckling, although whether he devised the game to provide a neutral space in which he and his father could co-exist without speaking is not recorded. Cribbage is often played in dark corners of pubs, by a father and son who would rather look at their cards – '*fifteen-two, fifteen-four, that's all there is, there ain't no more*' – than each other's faces. In Cribbage, a card game often played between a father and his son (now also a father himself) there are exactly 1,009,008 combinations of hands which score no points at all, while the top score possible with a single hand is 29. Although the game is often played in complete silence – by, say, a father and son who have long forgotten how to speak to each other – Cribbage nevertheless boasts its own rich glossary of phrases, like 'one for his nob' and 'two for his heels;' it has also given the English language such everyday expressions as 'pegging it' and 'streets ahead.' The card game Cribbage is most commonly played by two players, e.g. a father and the adult son he cannot bring himself to forgive. In this version, the winner is the first person to move his matchstick – or peg – up and down the Crib board twice, drain his pint glass, look at his watch and say, '*Aye, well...*'

About the Author

Originally from Manchester, Tim Craig lives in Hackney, London, with his wife and three children. He misspent his youth – and then some – writing radio commercials, and now allegedly works as a freelance copywriter. In 2018 he won the Bridport Prize for Flash Fiction and has placed or been commended four times in the Bath Flash Fiction Award. His short-short fiction has appeared in Best Microfictions 2019 & 2022, the BIFFY 50 list, and has also been nominated for Best Small Fictions and a Pushcart Prize. *Now You See Him* is Tim's first published collection of stories. You can find him on Twitter @timkcraig

Acknowledgements

Oof. Where to start?

Well, I started when my good friend, the writer Mandy Wheeler, suggested I try my hand at short-short fiction, so my first thanks go to her. Though I might not have carried on without the support and encouragement of Jude 'The Unflappable' Higgins at Ad Hoc Fiction, to whom I know many other writers also owe an enormous dollop of gratitude. Thank you to my vastly capable 'wing men' – Simon Petty and Tom Connolly – for their close reading of the stories, and their wise suggestions. Also to my sister, Jenny, for her excellent insight; to the phenomenal portrait artist Alan Coulson for the cover artwork, and to John at Ad Hoc Fiction for putting the whole thing together so brilliantly.

I'm hugely indebted to Christopher Allen, Fiona Mackintosh, Janice Leagra and Jude Higgins for their generous words on the back cover; thank you all so much. Also to the Flash Mob gang – the bestest, most supportive group of writers this side of Ougadougou. And to my parents Jess and Keith, who I hope would have been proud, despite the odd cameo appearance in the preceding pages (entirely fictional of course).

Finally, to my wife – and first reader – Susi, and to my children Florence, Boris and Annie. Couldn't do it without you.

Previously Published

Grateful thanks to the following anthologies and journals where these fictions were previously published:

Cat Barbecue – Atticus Review, January 2022

Going Down – Ellipsis Zine, September 2021 & Best Microfictions 2022

Incompatible – Splonk 5, April 2021

Northern Lights – Bath Flash Fiction Award, 3rd Place, June 2018 & Best Microfictions 2019

Now You See Him – Bath Flash Fiction Award, 3rd Place February 2021

Parts of My Mother – Milk Candy Review – January 2022

Planes, Horses and Planes – Bath Flash Fiction Award / With One Eye on the Cows

Riddle Me This – Bath Flash Fiction Award Longlist, February 2022.

That's All There Is, There Ain't No More – Bath Flash Fiction Award 3rd Place, September 2021

The Cake of her Life – Bath Flash Fiction Award / With One Eye on the Cows

The Falling Silent – Bath Flash Fiction Award, Commended, June 2019

The Grand Finale – Winner, Bridport Prize Flash Fiction, 2018